The
Playground
Problem

For the real Emma—M. M.

SIMON SPOTLIGHT
An imprint of Simon & Schuster Children's Publishing Division
1230 Avenue of the Americas, New York, NY 10020
This Simon Spotlight edition May 2022
First Aladdin Paperbacks edition April 2004
Text copyright © 2004 by Simon & Schuster, Inc.
Illustrations copyright © 2004 by Mike Gordon
SIMON SPOTLIGHT, READY-TO-READ, and colophon are
registered trademarks of Simon & Schuster, Inc.
For information about special discounts for bulk purchases,
please contact Simon & Schuster Special Sales at
1-866-506-1949 or business@simonandschuster.com.
Manufactured in the United States of America 0322 LAK
2 4 6 8 10 9 7 5 3 1
Cataloging-in-Publication Data was previously supplied for the paperback
edition of this title from the Library of Congress.
Library of Congress Cataloging-in-Publication Data
McNamara, Margaret.
The playground problem / by Margaret McNamara ;
illustrated by Mike Gordon.—1st Aladdin Paperbacks ed.
p. cm.—(Robin Hill School)
Summary: When first-graders Nick, Jamie, and Reza refuse to let Emma
join their soccer game just because she is a girl, Emma and her father
devise a plan to teach the boys a lesson.
[1. Sex role—Fiction. 2. Schools—Fiction. 3. Soccer—Fiction.]
I. Gordon, Mike, ill. II. Title.
PZ7.M47879343Pl 2004
[E]—dc21
2002155257
ISBN 978-1-6659-1369-0 (hc)
ISBN 978-0-689-85876-5 (pbk)
ISBN 978-1-4442-5792-8 (ebook)

The Playground Problem

Written by Margaret McNamara
Illustrated by Mike Gordon

Ready-to-Read

Simon Spotlight
New York   London   Toronto   Sydney   New Delhi

Monday was a sunny day.

It was recess.
Mrs. Connor's first-grade
class was on
the playground.

The boys were playing soccer.
"Hey!" called Emma.
"May I play?"

"No," said Nick.

"No," said Jamie.

"No," said Reza.

8

"We do not want you
to play with us,"
said Nick.

"Why not?" asked Emma.
"Because you are a girl,"
said Reza. "And girls
do not play soccer."

Emma was mad.

Emma was
very mad.

Emma was
FURIOUS.

That night she told her dad
all about the boys.

He helped her
figure out a plan.

On Tuesday
the girls ran out
to the playground.

They had a soccer ball.
They played soccer.

"Hey!" said Reza.

"The girls can play soccer."

"They are pretty good,"
said Nick.

"They are very good,"
said Jamie. "Emma! Come
and join the boys' team."

"No," said Emma.
"I do not want to play
on a team with just boys."

"Why not?" asked Nick.

"Figure it out," said Emma.

On Wednesday
it rained and rained.

The girls played
at the activity table.

The boys sat
and stared at the rain.

"What are they doing?"
asked Katie.
"They are figuring
it out," said Emma.

On Thursday
it was sunny again.
The girls were
scoring goals.

"Hey, Emma!" said Reza.
"We figured it out."

"Boys and girls
can play together,"
said Jamie.

"They can play
on the same team,"
said Reza.
"We got it," said Nick.

From then on,
the boys and girls played
together.

Sometimes they played
really well together.

Sometimes they had fights.

"I figure that
    playing together makes us
    the best team
    we can be," said Reza.

And he was right.

/